I0714428

It's almost Halloween, which is awful, because...

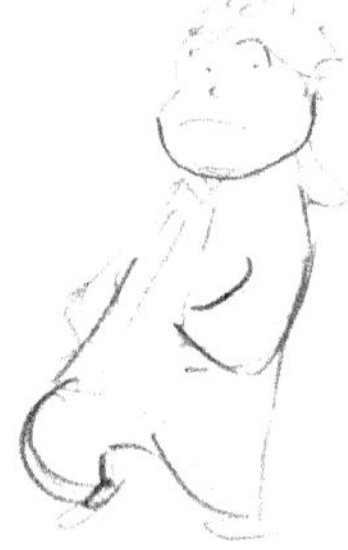

I'm Afraid of Aliens

I'm Bothered by Bats

I'm Cowed by Clowns

I'm Disturbed by Demons

I'm Edgy around Elves

I'm Frightened of Fairies

I'm Gutted by Ghosts

I'm Haunted by Homunculi

I'm Intimidated by Imps

I'm Jumpy around Jinn

I'm Kaput around Kappa

I'm Leery of Leprechauns

I'm Mistrusting of Mummies

I'm Nervous near Necromancers

I'm Oblivious to Ogres

I'm Petrified of Poltergeist

I'm Queasy around Quacks

I'm Ruined by Robots

I'm Suspicious of Spooky Spectral Skeletal Serpents

I'm Terrified of Tarantulas

I'm Upset by the Undead

I'm Vegetative near Vampires

I'm Worried by Werewolves

I'm Xenophobic of Xindhi

I'm Yellow around Yeti

But I'm positively Zealous about Zombies!

The End!

Dedicated to Christine Malek,
who terrorized me throughout grade school

It's Almost Halloween, Which Is Awful, Because...
a memoir by Polly Calavara about Perry Calavara

Stuff and whatever: © 2016, Never Knows Books

Originally published Oct 2015, one page per day, at Raccoonteurs.com, which is a thing we do that does that sort of thing, I guess.

ISBN: 978-0-9964120-7-0

Calavara.com   §   NeverKnows.com

NEVER
KNOWS
BOOKS